NEWMAN:
A STORY OF HOPE AND RESILIENCE

Newman James

DEDICATION

FOR THE VETERINARIANS WHO MENDED HIS BODY WITH STEADY HANDS, AND THE RESCUERS, SHELTERS, AND FOSTER FAMILIES WHO REFUSED TO GIVE UP — THANK YOU.

TO THE GOOD PEOPLE WHO RESCUE ABUSED ANIMALS: YOUR KINDNESS TURNS FEAR INTO HOPE.

FOR CHILDREN: REMEMBER TO BE GENTLE AND RESPECTFUL WHEN SOMEONE ISN'T PERFECT — EVERYONE DESERVES PATIENCE, KINDNESS, AND A CHANCE TO SHINE.

AND FOR MY BRAVE DOG — NOT DISABLED, BUT BEAUTIFULLY ENABLED — WHO TAUGHT US HOW TO LOVE WITH AN OPEN HEART. THIS BOOK IS FOR YOU.
NEWMAN

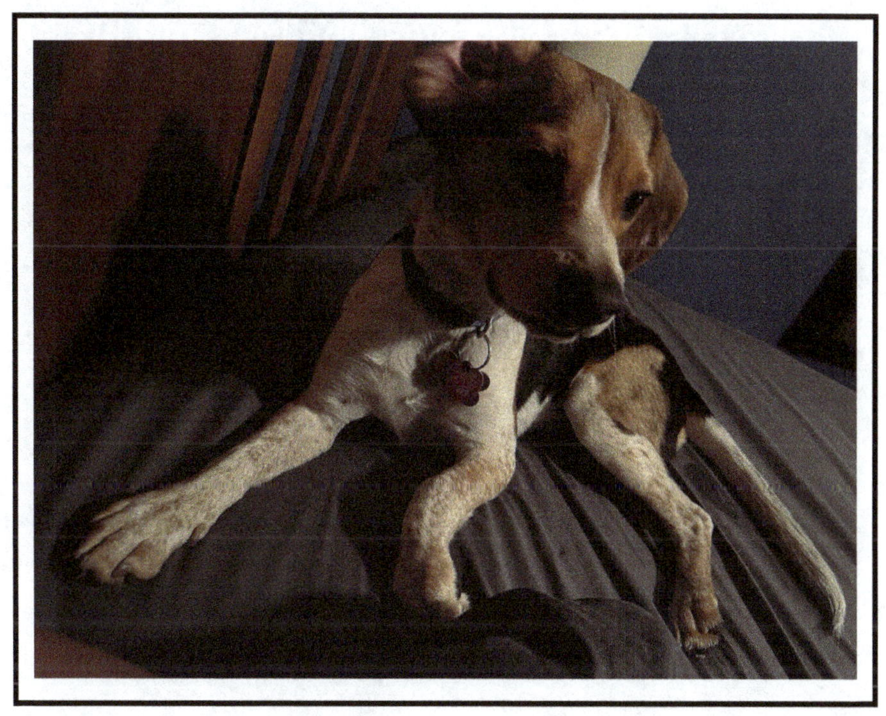

Newman

In a quiet neighborhood, Newman's story began with a tragic start. Found curled on the sidewalk beneath a flickering streetlamp, he was a small bundle of fur trembling with pain and cold. His breathing was shallow, and his hind leg was fractured and mangled beyond repair, evidence of a careless hit-and-run incident.

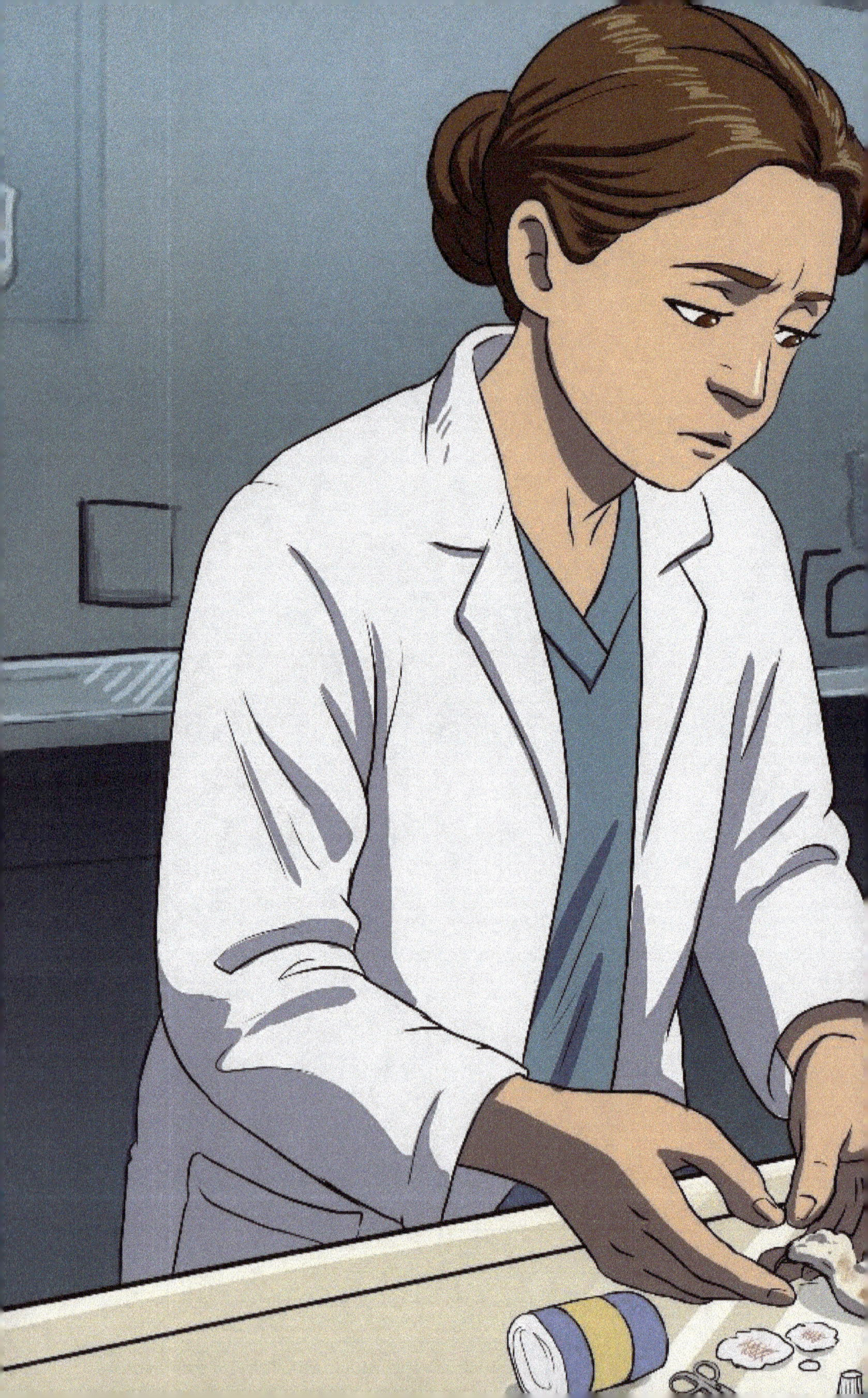

A compassionate neighbor promptly contacted animal rescue services. At the veterinary clinic, Newman's condition was assessed under harsh fluorescent lights, with the scent of antiseptic filling the air. The veterinarian examined him with gentle professionalism.

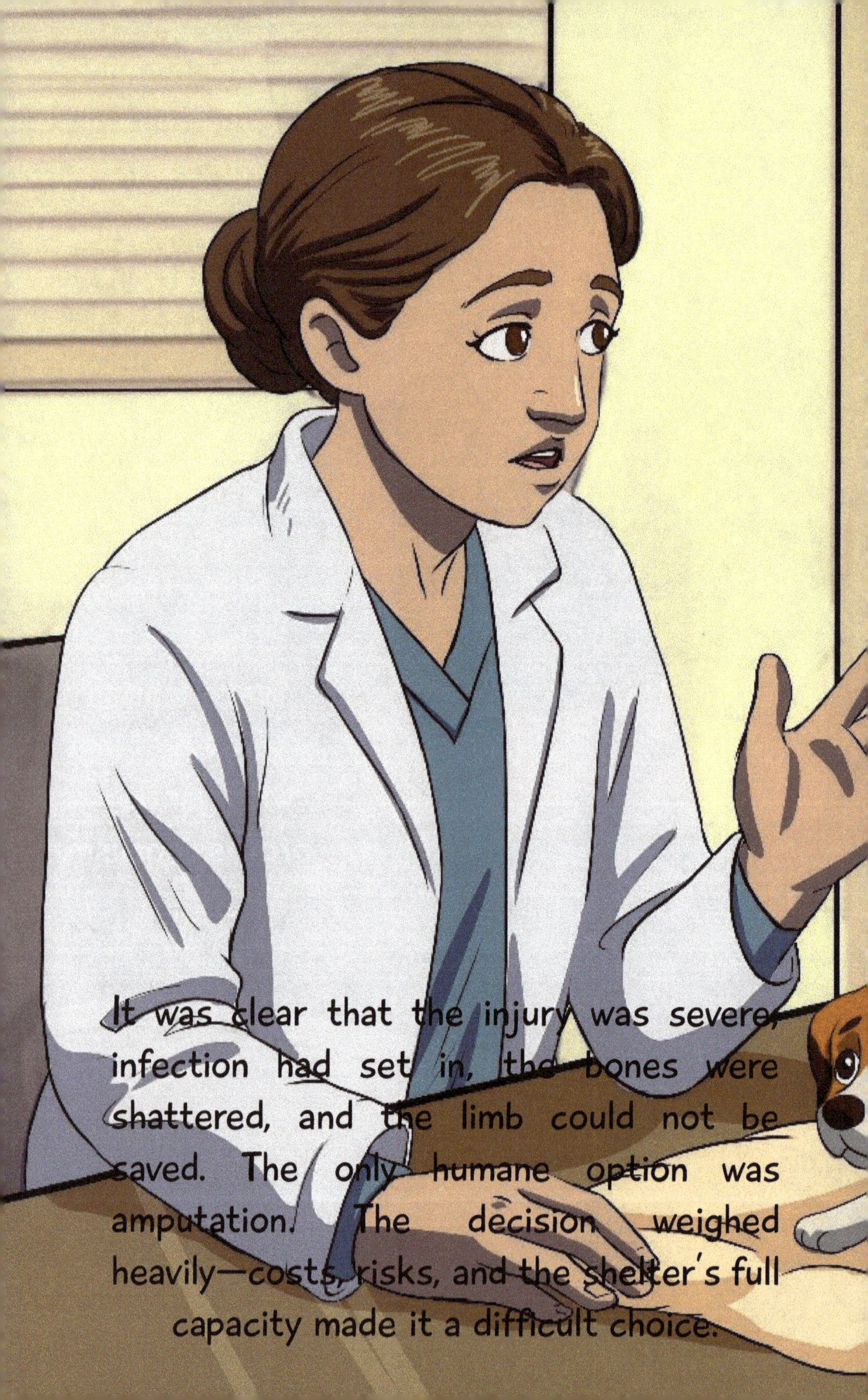

It was clear that the injury was severe, infection had set in, the bones were shattered, and the limb could not be saved. The only humane option was amputation. The decision weighed heavily—costs, risks, and the shelter's full capacity made it a difficult choice.

RESCUE

For several days, Newman, now officially named by those caring for him, was moved between different shelters, medicated, and kept warm. Despite his suffering, he found comfort in small things—a soft towel, the warmth of a heating lamp, and the kindness of strangers who paused to stroke his head.

Eventually, the veterinarian confirmed that amputation was necessary. Newman slept through the procedure, and upon awakening, he was greeted by a room that smelled of healing and disinfectant. He blinked blearily, realizing one of his hind legs was gone. The pain was significant, but something else stirred—an overwhelming sense of newness, bewilderment, and—gradually—trust in the hands that nurtured him.

News of Newman's plight reached a compassionate individual across town—a woman who could not ignore his soulful eyes and fragile condition. She quickly organized resources and reached out to her network.

A man with a kind heart, a small house, and two other dogs in need of love responded without hesitation: "I need him," he declared, recognizing the potential for a new beginning. On a bright, sunny afternoon, Newman was brought into his new home, wrapped gently in the arms of his rescuer, trembling but hopeful. His name was fitting—symbolic of renewal.

Initially, Newman moved cautiously, unfamiliar with his altered body. Stairs and porches posed challenges. However, with patience, love, and gentle guidance from his new furry family members, Newman adapted.

That evening, Newman met his new family for the very first time. His new mom immediately saw the gentle, loving dog inside the little guy who had been scared and hurt. He also met a brother, a playful, happy dog who greeted Newman with lots of barking and howling

Soon, the three of them were running, playing, barking, and howling together—all full of happiness. It was like they were meant to be a family from the very start.

Their happy noises filled the house and showed how hope, love, and a new beginning can happen when people and pets care for each other. Newman's story is a special reminder that with kindness and love, even the tiniest, most shy animals can find joy, friendship, and a forever home, where he sleeps peacefully at night with a paw draped affectionately over his new friend's tail.

Ramps were built, treats and praise encouraged him to use the doggy door, and small victories became milestones—balancing on three legs, chasing leaves across the yard. His resilience was remarkable. Despite his disability, Newman displayed a lively spirit.

He reveled in my lap and eagerly sought every opportunity for affection and play. His cautious nature softened over time, replaced by a carefree joy that warmed the hearts of everyone who met him.

His disability did not slow him down; instead, it highlighted his indomitable spirit and his ability to overcome adversity.

Newman's journey reflects the transformative power of compassion and hope. His story continues to inspire those around him, proving that with love and support, even the smallest and most vulnerable can find joy, belonging, and a fresh start.